Dear Beast #2

The Pet Parade

by DORI HILLESTAD BUTLER

illustrated by

KEVAN ATTEBERRY

HOLIDAY HOUSE • NEW YORK

For Bob. Sorry you couldn't have #1 this time. But you know you're always
#1 in my book. —D.H.B.

To my unlikely friends and friendships —K.A.

~~~~~~~~~~~~~~~~~~~~~~

Text copyright © 2021 by Dori Hillestad Butler   Illustrations copyright © 2021 by Kevan Atteberry
All Rights Reserved   HOLIDAY HOUSE is registered in the U.S. Patent and Trademark Office.
Printed and bound in October 2020 at Toppan Leefung, DongGuan, China   The artwork was created digitally with Photoshop.
www.holidayhouse.com   First Edition   1 3 5 7 9 10 8 6 4 2
Library of Congress Cataloging–in–Publication Data is available.
ISBN: 978–0–8234–4493–9 (hardcover)

CONTENTS

ONE
NICK NAME

FROM THE DESK OF

Simon

Dear Baxter,
   It has come to my attention that the city pet parade is coming up. I have marched in many parades with Andy. This year, as a sign of our new friendship, I would like to invite you to march in my place. What do you say?

Sincerely,
SIMON

I say: YAY!!!!!! PET PURRADE!!!!!!!!! And I alreddy noe abowt the purrade cuz Andy and Noah are mayking me a costoom. Hay, I thawt you were going to call me Beast! It's my nick name. But you need a nick name, too. And gess whut! I just thawt up the purrfekt one for you! Do you want to noe whut it is??? Huh? Do you? I'll tell you in my next letter. That is called keeping you in suspens! Hahahahahaha!!!!!

Luv and Liver Treats,
Beast

Simon

Dear Beast,

I do not need a nickname.

I am pleased to hear that you will be in the parade with Andy. That gives me time to catch up on some light reading.

Do let me know if I can help with the parade. And please check your spelling. I know you want to put your best paw forward.

Sincerely,
SIMON

Awww, come on! Evrywon needs a nick name. And I have a reelly, reelly good one for you!!!
I think you'll like it . . .
Are you reddy?
Wait for it . . .
Your new nick name is . . .
CAT MAN!!!!

Luv and Liver Treats,
Beast

FTS (Remember? That meens Fergot to Say.) Sorrry. No time to chek my speling rite now. I have to try on my costoom for the pet purrade. YAY!!!! PET PURRADE!!!!!

FROM THE DESK OF
Simon

Dear Beast,

Do not call me Cat Man! And for your information, it's p-a-r-a-d-e and c-o-s-t-u-m-e and e-v-e-r-y-o-n-e and r-e-a-l-l-y and—oh, never mind. There are <u>many</u> misspellings in your letter. Please try to do better next time.

Educationally yours,
SIMON

I'll try.
But speling
is hard. And
not vary fun.

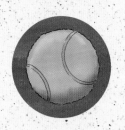

TWO

SIMON'S BOOKLET

FROM THE DESK OF

Simon

Dear Beast,

How are you? How is your costume for the pet parade? Don't be surprised if it's a bit uncomfortable. Costumes are like that. If I may ask, what is the costume?

Since you've never been in a parade before, I have taken the time to put together a little book to help you understand what is expected of you. Do let me know if you have any questions.

Helpfully yours,
SIMON

How to Be in a Parade

1. Do not bark.
2. Do not bite.
3. Do not pant.
4. Do not sniff.
5. Do not scratch.
6. Do not drool.
7. Do not pee.
8. Do not poop.
9. Do not pull.
10. Do not drag.
11. Do not meet.
12. Do not greet.
13. Do not eat.
14. Do not drink.

In summary, be on your best behavior at all times!

Dear CAT MAN,
  You fergot the most importint rool! You fergot: HAVE FUN!!!!!!

        Luv and Liver Treats,
        Beast

Simon

Dear Beast,
  Do NOT call me CAT MAN!
  And <u>you</u> forgot to tell me about your costume.

Curiously yours,
SIMON

I didn't ferget! I am keping
you in suspens! YAY!!!!
SUSPENS!!!! But my costoom is
reelly, reelly awsum!!!!! And it's
not uncomfterbull at all. Poor
Noah. He duzn't have a pet, so
he can't be in the purrade. I'm
glad I get to be in it. Too bad
you can't be in it, too!

FROM THE DESK OF
Simon

Dear Beast,
  This is not the time for suspense. When Andy came home from his dad's house yesterday, he seemed worried. I'm sure he wishes I was marching in the parade instead of you. But he'll be okay. We just need to show him that you are ready for the parade.

Seriously,
SIMON

P.S. I could be in the parade if I wanted to be in it.

Dear Cat Man,

 I'm todally reddy for the purrade! YAY!!!! PET PURRADE!!!!! And Andy's not wurried abowt me. He's wurried about Soffy Snikrman and the Terryer Twins!

Luv and Liver Treats,
Beast

19

Sophie Snickerman

THREE

TRYING TO HELP

FROM THE DESK OF

Simon

Dear Bubbles,

How are you, old friend? I am writing about the pet parade. You've probably heard that Baxter will be marching this year instead of me. Have you, by any chance, had a look at his costume? I just want to check in and make sure he's taking the parade seriously.

Sincerely,
SIMON

Blub . . .

Blub . . .

Dear Simon,

"Old friend"? *Blub . . . blub . . .* You think we're friends? *Blub . . . blub . . .* Let's keep our relationship professional, shall we? *Blub . . . blub . . .*

To answer your question, yes, I have seen Baxter's costume. *Blub . . . blub . . .* It's fantastic! *Blub . . . blub . . .* That Noah sure has interesting ideas! *Blub . . . blub . . .*

Who are you to talk about not taking the parade seriously? *Blub . . . blub . . .* Remember last year? *Blub . . . blub . . .* I still don't know what happened, *blub . . . blub . . .* but I'm sure it was your fault. *Blub . . . blub . . .* You were trying to get out of the parade all along! *Blub . . . blub . . .* But you didn't get out of it. *Blub . . . blub . . .* And then suddenly I had to be in it, too. *Blub . . . blub . . .*

I tried to make the best of it. *Blub . . . blub . . .*

I tried to be a good fish. *Blub . . . blub . . .*
But were you a good Cat in the Hat?
Blub . . . blub . . . No, you were not. *Blub . . .*
blub . . . Isn't it nice that Baxter's going to
be in the parade this year instead of you?
Blub . . . blub . . . Dogs are so much better at
parades than cats are.

Not your friend,
Blub . . . blub . . . blub . . .
BUBBLES

FROM THE DESK OF
Simon

Dear Bubbles,

    Let's not talk about last year's parade.

    I want you to know, Bubbles, that I have always thought of you as a friend. But if you prefer to keep our relationship professional, I will respect your wishes.

    As one professional to another, please allow me to share some information. Dogs have no pride. They do things that no self—respecting cat would ever do. As a result, they may, for a moment, _appear_ to be better than cats, but they are NOT better. Do you understand the difference between appearing better and actually being better?

    Now please tell me what Baxter will be wearing in the parade.

Respectfully yours,
SIMON

Blub . . .

Blub . . .

Dear Simon,

Sorry, Noah says Andy's and Baxter's costumes are a secret! *Blub . . . blub . . .* You know how Sophie Snickerman and the Terrier Twins always win first prize in the costume contest? *Blub . . . blub . . .* It's not fair. Her mom works at a costume store! *Blub . . . blub . . .* Well, they aren't going to win this year. You know why? *Blub . . . blub . . .* Because Noah has been giving Andy and Baxter acting lessons! *Blub . . . blub . . .* Andy and Baxter aren't just dressing up as fun characters. They're learning how to act like those characters! *Blub . . . blub . . .* That Noah sure is smart!

Your friend,
Blub . . . blub . . . blub . . .
BUBBLES

P.S. If you and I ever see each other again, you know it would be UNPROFESSIONAL of you to eat me, don't you? *Blub . . . blub . . .*

FROM THE DESK OF
Simon

Dear Bubbles,

   I am hurt that you still think I might eat you. You know how I feel about getting my nose wet. Let's move on.

   Please know that as Andy's longtime and beloved pet, I am here to help him and Baxter. They don't need Noah.

   Tell me who Andy and Baxter are dressing up as. Please.

Trying to help,
SIMON

Blub . . .

Blub . . .

Dear Simon,

   You seem stressed. *Blub . . . blub . . .* A little yoga might help you relax. *Blub . . . blub . . .* Don't worry about Andy and Baxter. They're fine. *Blub . . . blub . . .* And don't worry about the parade. Everything is under control.

                    Blub . . . blub . . . blub . . .
                    BUBBLES

F O U R
CAT MAN

FROM THE DESK OF
Simon

Dear Stinky,
   How are you? How is the family? I am well.
   You may or may not know that Baxter is marching in this year's pet parade instead of me. I wonder if you might do me a small favor. You pass through Andy's dad's yard now and then. Could you find out what Baxter will be wearing in the parade?
   Thank you for your time.

Sincerely,
SIMON

FROM THE DESK OF
Simon

Dear Stinky,

Did you get my letter? Why haven't you written back? This is an urgent matter. The parade is coming up soon!

Thank you for your time.

With concern,
SIMON

Dear Cat Man,

I didn't know you cared so much about the pet parade. Remember last year, you asked me to spray your costumes? Too bad. You would've made a great taco and Andy would've made a great cook!

I think it's wonderful that Baxter is going to be in the parade. I haven't seen his costume. That's why I haven't written. I've been trying to peek in through the patio door, but you know I don't see very well. I'll keep trying, but you might want to ask Cheeks if he's seen anything. He's been up in the tree outside Andy's window, and his eyes are better than mine. I'd ask him myself, but he tends to stay away from me. I can't imagine why.

Yours truly,

STINKY

FROM THE DESK OF

Simon

Dear Cheeks,

   How are you? I hope you have a nice supply of nuts for the winter.

   I hear you've been spending some time in the tree outside Andy's window. Have you, by any chance, seen Baxter's costume for the pet parade? Please tell me what it is.

Sincerely,
SIMON

Dear Cat Man,

I've seen the costumes, but I don't know who Baxter and Andy are supposed to be. Noah comes over every day and helps them act out their parts. Andy is a good actor! I think Baxter just likes getting dressed up. You know, for a dog, he's not half bad. He just wants to make Andy happy.

Best,
CHEEKS

FROM THE DESK OF

Simon

Dear Snail,

First, I'd like to say thank you for delivering all of my mail. I really appreciate your efforts.

The next time you're in Baxter's neighborhood, would you crawl up the side of the house and see if you can find out who Baxter and Andy are going to be in the parade?

Thank you for your time.

Sincerely,
SIMON

FIVE
FOR A PRICE

FROM THE DESK OF
Simon

Dear Beast,

Everyone is calling me Cat Man! Did you tell them to do that? Please stop.

Now, tell me about your costume. I really must know what it is!

Firmly,
SIMON

Where is that Snail?

Dear Cat Man,

I understand you have a letter to be delivered. Snail is busy. But I can deliver mail. For a price . . .

Signed,
EDGAR ALLAN CROW

Simon
to: Beast

Dear Cat Man,

   Really? That's all you have to offer? A dirty old penny? It's not even a shiny penny. This must not be a very important letter.

                    Signed,
                        EDGAR ALLAN CROW

Much better.

Dear Cat Man,

You are a good deetektive! Yup! I'm the one who told evrywon to call you Cat Man. You may not noe this but sum fokes think yor a little unfrendly. I thawt a nick name wood help you have more frends! YAY!!! FRENDS!!!!!! And Cat Man makes you sownd like a sooper hero. Don't you want to be a sooper hero?

Luv and Liver Treats,
Beast

Simon

Dear Beast,

   No. I do not wish to be a superhero. Superheroes are silly. My hero is Sherlock Holmes. There is nothing silly about him. This is the last time I'm going to ask you about your costume. If you don't tell me what it is, I will be forced to escape my house and come see it for myself. I would hate to have to do that. What will everyone think if they see me out and about? They'll think I'm a common tomcat who doesn't have a family to serve him! I will have to inform them that my boy has a dog who is completely out of control.

Seriously,

SIMON

Dear Cat Man,

I've seen Baxter's costume. I'll tell you what it is, for a price . . .

Signed,

EDGAR ALLAN CROW

Dear Cat Man,

Baxter is going to be Sherlock Hound in the pet parade. And Andy is going to be Sherlock Hound's loyal sidekick, Watson. You should see their costumes. They're going to win a shiny prize in the parade for sure! You and Andy never won a prize, did you? You always had your costume half off by the end of the parade. I heard this is the last time Andy can be in the pet parade. Next year he'll be too old. Good thing he gets to be in it with Baxter instead of you, huh?

Signed,
EDGAR ALLAN CROW

SIX
NOPE

FROM THE DESK OF
Simon

Dear Beast,

   This letter is to inform you that your services in the pet parade are no longer required. I will march in the parade after all. Please place your costume inside Andy's backpack. I will get it when Andy returns to my house, and I will wear it in the parade. Thank you.

Sincerely,
SIMON

Simon

Dear Beast,

What do you mean, "nope"? Don't you understand? You don't have to be in the parade anymore. You can stay home and watch TV with Bubbles. Doesn't that sound like fun? I know how you enjoy your fun.

Sincerely,
SIMON

Dear Cat Man,

Reelly? You don't noe what nope meens? It meens NO! You can't have my costoom. It's a Shirlock Hownd costoom and Shirlock Hownd is a dog. You are a cat! But I'm glad you want to be in the purrade with Andy and me. YAY!!!! PET PURRADE!!!!! Maybee Andy and Noah can make you anuther costoom. Maybee you can be Shirlock Hownd's wife. Or maybee you can preetend yor Noah's pet and you giys can have todally diffrint costooms. Then Noah can be in the purrade, too.

Luv and Liver Treats,
Beast

Simon

Dear Beast,

I am not going to pretend I'm Noah's pet. That is ridiculous.

And Sherlock Holmes does not have a wife.

I will be Sherlock Cat, not Sherlock Dog. I will march in the parade and you will stay home. That is final! Now, put the costume in Andy's suitcase. Do it now so you don't forget.

Determinedly,
SIMON

Nope.

And it's HOWND,

not dog. Shirlock Hownd,

Dog Deetektive!

UNDERCOVER

Dear Cat Man Simon,

   Thank you for your letter. I was so happy to receive it. I was also happy to spy on Baxter and Andy for you. Did you know I've always wanted to be a spy? I was able to obtain the intelligence you requested. Baxter and Andy are wearing Sherlock Hound and Watson costumes!

Undercover,

SNAIL

Simon

Dear Snail,

Yes, I know that the beast and Andy have Sherlock Holmes and Watson costumes! However, I should be in the parade instead of Beast. Let's be honest. Cats are smarter than dogs. Therefore, a Sherlock Cat costume makes a lot more sense than a Sherlock Dog costume. But the beast won't give up the costume. How do I make him?

Sincerely,
SIMON

Dear Cat Man Simon,

   I don't understand. Why do you even want to be in the parade? You hate parades. You hate everything about them. Especially the costumes. Are you . . . jealous of Baxter?

Undercover,
SNAIL

FROM THE DESK OF
Simon

Dear Snail,
   No. I am not.

                    Confidently,
                    SIMON

Dear Cat Man Simon,

I didn't think so. So, let me ask you again.
Why do you want to be in the parade? You
must have a reason. If it's a good reason, you
should tell Baxter. Maybe he'll step aside.
IF you ask nicely. Think about it.

Your friend,
SNAIL

FROM THE DESK OF

Simon

Dear Beast,

I would like to be in the parade because . . . well, because Andy and I have been in many parades together, but we have never won a prize. That could be, in part, because . . . well, never mind. This is the last year Andy can be in the parade and I would really like to beat that Sophie Snickerman and the Terrier Twins! If I am dressed as my personal hero, Sherlock Holmes, perhaps Andy and I will be able do that. Would you let us try? I'll let you call me Cat Man . . .

Sincerely,

SIMON, the Cat Man

Dear Cat Man,

I undirstand, but gess whut? I alreddy call you Cat Man!!!!

I think I shud be in the purrade. Cuz I reelly, reelly, reelly want to be in it. And you sed I cud be in it. You sed it was a sine of our frend ship. You can't take back a sine of frend ship.

Hay! How abowt I give you a sine of our frend ship, too! Heer! You can have my ball! Now I get to be in the purrade insted of you, rite? YAY!!!! PET PURRADE!!!!!

Luv and Liver Treats,
Beast

Dear Cat Man,

I understand you'd like Baxter's costume. I can get it for you. For a price . . .

Signed,
EDGAR ALLAN CROW

EIGHT
THE PARADE

FROM THE DESK OF

Simon

Dear Edgar Allan Crow,
Thank you for your kind offer, but I am not in
need of your services at this time.

Sincerely,
SIMON

Simon

Dear Beast,

    After much consideration, I have decided to allow you to march in the pet parade. Please read the book I gave you. Memorize it! Since this is the last time Andy will be in the parade, we want things to go well. We also want you and Andy to beat Sophie Snickerman.
Good luck!

Yours,
SIMON

Dear Cat Man,
    I won't let you down!

            Luv and Liver Treats,
            Beast

Simon

Dear Beast,

Do not call me Cat Man. You may recall, I said you could call me Cat Man if I marched in the parade. Now that I have chosen not to march, the offer is no longer valid.

Yours,
SIMON

Dear Simon,
 Fine. I'll call you Simon. And look, I even speled it rite, didn't I?
 Enyway . . . did you watsh the purrade? Huh? Did you? Did you? Andy and I had SO much fun. And did you see? We even won first prize! YAY!!!!
        Luv and Liver Treats,
            Beast

FROM THE DESK OF

Simon

Dear Beast,

I did watch the parade. And I'm sorry to tell you this, but you and Andy did not win <u>first</u> prize. Sophie Snickerman and the Terrier Twins did. You and Andy won second prize. Oh, well. At least you had fun, right? Andy certainly did. He had much to say about it afterward.

Yours,

SIMON

Dear Simon,

YAY!!!! SECOND PRIZE!!!!!

And yes, I had tuns of fun! Hay! Aren't you glad we beelong to Andy insted of Soffy Snikrman? When it comes to hyoomans we got a way better prize than the Terryier Twins got. Cuz we got Andy!

Luv and Liver Treats,
Beast

FROM THE DESK OF
Simon
~~~~~~~~~

Dear Beast,
You are right about that.

Fondly,
SIMON

DOGGY DICTIONARY

abowt = about
alreddy = already
anuther = another

beelong = belong

chek = check
costoom = costume
cud = could
cuz = because

deetektive = detective
diffrint = different
duzn't = doesn't

enyway = anyway
evrywon = everyone

ferget = forget
fergot = forgot
fokes = folks
frend ship = friendship
frends = friends
FTS = Forgot to Say

gess = guess
giys = guys

hay = hey
heer = here
hownd = hound
hyooman(s) = human(s)

importint = important
insted = instead

keping = keeping

luv = love

maybee = maybe
mayking = making
meens = means

nick name = nickname
noe = know

preetend = pretend
purrade = parade
purrfekt = perfect

reddy = ready
reelly = really
rite = write or right
rool/rools = rule/rules

sed = said
Shirlock = Sherlock
shud = should
sine = sign
sooper = super
sorrry = sorry
sownd = sound
speled = spelled
speling = spelling
sum = some
suspens = suspense

terryier = terrier
thawt = thought
todally = totally
tuns = tons
uncomfterbull =
    uncomfortable
unfrendly = unfriendly

vary = very

watsh = watch
whut = what
wood = would
wurried = worried

yor = you're